Augusta De Gruchy

**Under the Hawthorn and Other Verse**

Augusta De Gruchy

**Under the Hawthorn and Other Verse**

ISBN/EAN: 9783337279479

Printed in Europe, USA, Canada, Australia, Japan

Cover: Foto ©Andreas Hilbeck / pixelio.de

More available books at **www.hansebooks.com**

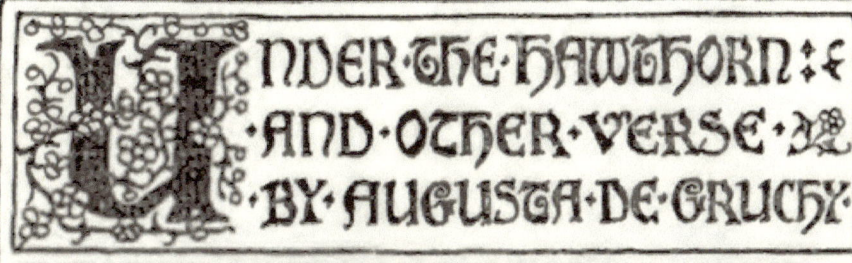

Under the Hawthorn :
and other verse :
by Augusta de Gruchy

London: Elkin Mathews & John Lane
at the Bodley Head in Vigo St. 1893

# CONTENTS.

| | PAGE |
|---|---|
| To Maud Irene | 1 |
| Under the Hawthorn | 2 |
| Polly | 5 |
| Dreams | 9 |
| By the Brook | 13 |
| The Old Garden | 16 |
| Amabel to her Husband | 18 |
| Spring's Delays | 20 |
| Life | 22 |
| I. N. take thee M. | 23 |
| A Little Day | 24 |
| At a Dance | 25 |
| Evening Reflections | 27 |
| Dulces Amaryllidis Iræ | 28 |
| The Pity of it | 29 |
| Rêves D'Antan | 30 |
| The Seasons | 31 |
| In the Churchyard | 33 |
| A Sealed Letter | 35 |
| To One in Italy | 37 |

|  | PAGE |
|---|---|
| To One in England | 38 |
| Flower of Love | 39 |
| Moribunda | 40 |
| To Crystal | 42 |
| Grief's Philosophy | 44 |
| Moira | 46 |
| Lily | 47 |
| Amaranth | 48 |
| Beyond these Voices | 49 |
| A White Violet | 52 |
| In a Lighthouse | 54 |
| Arrêts D'Amour | 60 |
| Riduna Lys | 65 |
| The Poet to a Lady | 68 |
| Madonna | 69 |
| My Household Goddess | 70 |
| Love and Death | 71 |
| The Peacemaker | 72 |
| A Hand at Whist | 74 |
| Should Amy Waltz | 75 |
| This Book of mine | 76 |
| I was a Rosebud in June | 77 |
| This Day | 79 |
| Pastor Bonus | 80 |
| The Soul's Temple | 81 |
| Earth Notes | 84 |
| The Dregs of the Cup | 85 |

## TO MAUD IRENE.

May these long prisoned fancies now take wing,
   And, swiftly speeding over miles of sea
Unto thy distant dwelling, sing to thee,
Dear, earliest blossom of my life's glad spring!


If crude their notes, like those of some tame bird
Recaptured after loss, that tries repeat
Every new trill and quaver that he heard
Near stranger nests, yet use may make them sweet:
Enough.   Fit thou to each poor air its word.

# UNDER THE HAWTHORN.

"WHEN the white blossoms on the hawthorn tree
     Give place to haws, or ever these be red,
The little babe I hold upon my knee
     Will walk alone, reluctant to be led:

"Later, will run, blind to my warning finger,
     Here, in the field, where flashes the swift scythe
O'er the shorn turf that tempts the foot to linger;
     (Could mother happier be or boy more blithe?)

"Will run; I'll chase him round the tree's rough bole;
     Hold up, brave laddie!  Trip not, I beseech!
Caught!  Of my captive I demand full toll,
     Then toss him, laughing, high as arm can reach.

"Toss him so high that myriad flying things
　　With flutter of wing, start from their leafy lair,
While baby claps his hands, and crows, and sings,
　　And plucks dropt petals out of mother's hair.


" Winter will come : the song-birds' time of woe ;
　　For them our hawthorn ripens his good fruit,
While winds blow keen, and feathery rime and snow
　　Drape his bare twigs and heap about his root.


" Winter will come.　Will baby care ?　Not he !
　　To romp with mother in her cosy den,
Or hear her read, close pressed against her knee,
　　Is surely joy enough for little men.


" Then Spring will follow fast.　Finches will build,
　　The garrulous wrens will chatter as they mate ;
Spring will revive what winter almost killed,
　　And sweet surprises on our footsteps wait."

She ended and sat silent, with bowed head
  Clasping her darling closer to her breast;
Then, issuing from the hawthorn's ample shade,
  Onward she passed, hushing the babe to rest.

\*    \*    \*    \*

Winter has come.   No blossom decks the bough.
  Fair life !   must *you* too with the bloom depart ?
O, what is left of all May's promise now ?
  Some scattered berries, and an aching heart.

# POLLY.

THERE is the old stone house, with its porch by
    ivy o'ershaded;
  Ivy that droops like the hair on my long-ago lost
    love's face:
Wretched, too wretched am I to enter, too way-worn
    and jaded;
  Yet even an outcast like me may *look* at the dear
    old place.


Back swings the gate....We were sweethearts;
    'twas always "Harry and Polly"
  As children, and lovers we were when I came unto
    man's estate;
But my father discouraged my fancy and swore that
    a young fool's folly
  Was curable only by banishment far from the
    young fool's mate.

I went.  Was it fate, bad luck, or something God
    sent to pursue me,
  Hunted me after I left her ?—will hunt to my
    latest breath—
Shipwreck, marsh-fever, a wound from an enemy's
    hand that nigh slew me,
  Letters from England that told of poverty, sickness
    and death.


Death !  but not hers.... That's her room ;  there
    where a glimmer of fire is :
  Nay, 'tis the red-screened lamp that she lit when
    I used to come
Up through the roses at dusk.... Is yonder blue
    flower the great iris,
  Whose bulb I uprooted and sent from a garden-
    plot hard by Rome ?


How soft the dew falls !.... Had I stayed, I wonder
    how I had repaid her

Her love ? Not so ill, as it seems to a soul with
    misfortune grown big ;
Yet—graces so many I lack ; unhappy I might have
    made her ;
  The willow-tree yields not the olive ; the ilex
    bears not the fig.


I'll close the gate gently and go.... home ? Why, I
    boast but a " dwelling "
  In a sordid street of the city, where faces are
    scamed with despair ;
Where the paving-stone artist sits patient, and street-
    singers' hearts are swelling,
  As they warble of breezes and brooks, in the dust
    and the drouth and the glare.


Hark ! there are steps on the gravel.... a voice....
    two voices .... " O, *Harry !* "
  (Her sisters') " Come in. What joy ! We have
    missed you this many a year :

And Polly, she *knew* you would come; they could
    never persuade her to marry."
  Lo! Surely the heavens are opened, and these are
    the angels I hear.


Dreams and delusions! They pass. A stranger's
    the dear old place is;
  Voices from dreamland were those I heard in that
    welcoming shout;
Even lov'd faces are fading. O, stay for one
    moment, ye faces!
  They vanish. I turn from the gate as the rose-
    shaded lamp dies out.

# DREAMS.

## IN THE PRISON VAN.

*T*RULY, *the light is sweet*, the wise man says,
     And *pleasant is it to behold the sun;*
Under these trees, that temper its fierce rays,
  A man might sit and dream till day were done.


Who cried, "Awake!" Oh! there you are, my pair
  Of treasures, worth all else below Heav'n's dome:
My brave boy, Frank, and my demure wife, Clare;
  No man more blest than I in wife and home.


Church, did you say? See! how that sunbeam creeps
  Thro' those young leaves. One gets a clearer **sense**,
Here, of God's works than where your curate heaps
  Platitudes up that pass for eloquence.

Heav'n seems less distant underneath this beech
    Than 'mid four walls—nay, dear one, look not vext;
Stoop, Clare! Come, boy! that's well; an arm for each;
    Now, fresh from church, repeat, forthwith, the text.


*Shall not the Judge of all the earth do right?*
    Judge! would you mock me? (whence this sudden
        pain?)
My brain spins round; the bright day turns to night;
    My limbs are lead. Help! do I dream again?


That man I envy whom no enemy
    Slanders in secret—scattering wide a store
Of poison-seeds for sprouting by and bye—
    As mine did; till who loved me, love no more.


Wife! let me feel your hand. My head, you know
    Is something strange since that black, dreadful day
When one, whose name we breathe not, struck a blow
    That threatened our fair home in dust to lay.

Great God! Could I endure it? Blow for blow
   Was surely righteous. Nay—my wild mood flies.
Look up, love! See! I crush the serpent; so!
   It shall not mar our perfect Paradise.


Come, Frank, produce your news! The chestnut bloom
   Is out? The colt begins to bark the trees?
Old Cowslip's calf is thriving? John, the groom,
   Has saved a bull-pup for you, if *I* please?


I know the wren—do I?—in yonder thick
   Ivy-clad wall; her eggs are unhatched still?
Enough! who's for a walk—Frank, fetch my stick!—
   Round by the lonely beacon on the hill?


Stop! the child's hand is red!....not blood!....(Oh God!
   That leaden weight!) Speak! Speak! and make an end!
A leveret snared....stretched dead upon the sod?
   Boy! you forget your lesson....*ne'er to blend*....

What are the lines? (He might have scoured this stain;
  Hare's blood, not man's; that's harder far to cleanse)
Help! help! my chair is moving....(Oh! this pain!)
  Come! the quotation—not the words, the sense!


You cannot? Quick! my Wordsworth!....On I glide,
  Or seem to glide, as if my chair had wheels....
Read! *Ne'er to blend our pleasure or our pride*
  *With sorrow of the meanest thing that feels.*


Sweet wife! Forgive my past wild mood, and think
  Its strangeness sprung from a disordered brain,
Stay near me, love! to please you I will drink
  The wine you bring me; then—to sleep again!


My chair stands still. How deadly cold it seems
  Here, on the lawn. (Again, that crushing weight!)
Who touched me? Clare! did you?—to end my dreams?
  I wake. Good God! What's here? THE PRISON GATE.

## BY THE BROOK.

FAREWELL! full many a coming Spring,
    Shall see you walk the brookside way,
To ears not mine low whispering
    New vows.   Old vows, ah! where are they?


Hear my last prayer! my last in life;
    Raise from that other's breast your head:
I die.   You should have been my wife.
    Wait *till* I die before you wed.


Recall the past!  Come, tread, once more,
    The ground you trod of old with me;
Drink in the fragrance from the shore;
    Hear the low murmur of the sea.

Trace once again the path we took
　　While still the tardy ash-buds slept,
And o'er our heads, beside the brook,
　　In palest green the willow wept.


How sweet the thousand childish ways
　　Wherewith to while an idle hour;
To plait the grasses, weave the sprays
　　Of traveller's joy and honey-flower!


Rather I woo the memory calm
　　Of eves when, silent for love's sake,
I heard you speak of vine and palm;
　　Of seas whereon no billows break;


Of tropic flowers; fair, fragile toys,
　　Made for the childhood of the world.
" We three," you said, " shall taste those joys."
　　" What three ? " I asked.　Your proud lip curled

In feigned derision ;  " Love," you said,
  " And you, and I ; we'll try that land."
Poor three !  *You* live, but Love is dead ;
  And here, O God ! a wreck *I* stand.


Yet, go in peace !  Since you must wed,
  (I would not have you lonely dwell)
Wait till they tell you I am dead,
  And take forgiveness with farewell.

# THE OLD GARDEN.

No change, you say? nothing of loss that tells?
  Trees, flowers, are they as lovely as of yore?
Does Spring still deck with corals and green bells
  Our favourite sycamore?


The early lilacs, bloom they rank on rank,
  Purple, and white, as they have bloomed for years?
Old Crown-Imperial on the mossy bank,
  Sheds he his hoarded tears?


The rose-acacia, does it carpet now
  The pathway with its waxen blossoms red?
Drop the smooth berries from the laurel bough
  Into the violet bed?

Suffer the birds no loss, bereft so **long**
   Of us ?   Is not the blackbird mute for doubt ?
Is no part wanting to the thrush's **song** ?
   No liquid note left out ?


**Does the moon** show behind the hedgerow-elms,
   Black bars against a spectral sea of light ?
Reigns our one star over the heavenly realms
   King, on a clear, cold night ?


They bloom, sing, shine ; our absence hindering not:
   They are but waiting till ourselves have ranged
**Enough,** so we, revisiting that spot,
   May find them all unchanged.

# AMABEL TO HER HUSBAND.

ALL may be well with us once more.  You love me,
    Or so you sware long since with book and bell;
Have you but patience and the will to prove me,
    All may be well.


All may be well.  Try me, take me to task, it
    Will not be hard to storm my citadel;
Scale my high walls! break down my forts!  I ask it;
    All may be well.


All may be well.  I was in fault; fool-hardy,
    I dashed against your calm invincible,
Then fell back spent.  Take my regrets, tho' tardy;
    All may be well.

**All** may be well.   Selfish my love, **I own** it ;
   Love such as mine soon rings Love's funeral knell.
Henceforth my flame burns clearer than you've known it :
   **All may** be well.


**All may be** well.   **Mine was** the fault ; believe it.
   Still silent ?   Here's your ring.   *To Amabel,*
Engraved inside.   What ! will you not receive it ?
   **All may be** well.


All may be well.   **How** easily can wedded
   Hands clasp once more, lips their old tales re-tell ;
Love can avert the lonely doom **we dreaded** :
   All may be well.


All may be well.   Replace Love's golden fetter ;
   **Rivet it** fast ; my wavering mind compel.
Teach me to love self less, to know you better ;
   All may be well.

Beauty of buds that blow!  Sorrow of flowers that
      fall !
April herself is a cheat, since none of her gifts abide :
Did she inherit from March a wind that her firstlings
      slew,
Daffodils, fugitive, frail, a wind that scattered them all?
Snapping their delicate stems—so cruel the blast it
      blew—
Laying the pasque-flower low, the primrose dead at its
      side ;
Till even the self-sown tuft of wallflower hardy and tall,
Wedged in a chink of the granite, that many a gust
      defied,
Mingled a hint of decay with its splendid wine-dark
      hue.

All is not over yet.  Valerian fringes the wall ;
Ferns spring thick in the bank the primrose ruin to
    hide,
And see I in the hedge-gap yonder, just where the sky
    shows blue,
There where the ivy climbs, and the bryony boughs
    divide,
One little stitchwort star, hope of the spring, shines
    through.

# LIFE.

Dream of the darkness that dies with the morn
    like a tropical flower !
  Thy past, too far for recall, as a bird from the hand
    has fled;
Thy shadowy future we see not; brief, brief is the
    vanishing hour,
  And the touch that awakes us at dawn at sunset may
    straighten us, dead.

## I, N, TAKE THEE, M.

Nor gold, nor lands, nor beauty that controls
    Man's heart, were mine; I brought not even
      health
Our home to bless. Love only came with me,
Love, that met yours and doubled. All our wealth
Was that harmonious blending of two souls,
    Which we call sympathy.

# A LITTLE DAY.

A LITTLE day!
    From rosy morn to evening grey;
A waiting day, a day of fear;
Of listening for a footfall dear
That comes not—nay, that nevermore
Shall sound upon our chamber floor:
Yet live we out as best we may
Our little day.

## AT A DANCE.

My Queen is tired and craves surcease
   Of twanging string and clamorous brass;
I lean against the mantelpiece,
  And watch her in the glass.


One whom I see not where I stand
  Fans her, and talks in whispers low;
Her loose locks flutter as his hand
  Moves lightly to and fro.


He begs a flower; her finger-tips
  Stray round a rose half veiled in lace;
She grants the boon with smiling lips,
  Her clear eyes read his face.

I cannot look—my sight grows dim—
　While Fate allots, unequally,
The living woman's self to him,
　The mirrored form to me.

# EVENING REFLECTIONS.

*After* Horace.

CHILD, I detest your dress ; my anger rises
  At rasping silks, at waists of eighteen inches ;
Cease buying at the shop that advertises
  The gown that pinches !


Wear flowing muslins, nothing else, I bid you,
Or softest woollens if the sky be fretful ;
Good-night ! sleep well, and, that I ever chid you,
  Awake forgetful.

## DULCES AMARYLLIDIS IRÆ.

I TOLD my love a truth she liked not well ;
  She spoke no word :  I raised my eyes to watch
Her cheek's red flush, her bosom's angry swell ;
  She rose to go ;  her hand was on the latch ;
When some swift thought—of my fond love, maybe,
  Or ill-requited patience—bowed her head :
She faltered, paused with foot half raised to flee,
  Then turned, and stole into my arms instead.

# "THE PITY OF IT!"

*The remembrance of past joy is present sorrow's
sharpest sting.*

O WONDROUS thought! mighty, and old and sad;
   Mighty as death, and old as the old world,
And sad as love that was and is no more;
Dug, in dead days, like diamond from the mine,
Out of a Roman prisoner's wealthy brain;
Chosen, long ages afterwards, to blaze
The central light of Dante's diadem;
And last, caught up by one whose heavenly crown
But late displaced the laurel; his hand raised
And set this jewel mid those other gems
" That on the stretch'd forefinger of all Time
" Sparkle for ever!"

# RÊVES D'ANTAN.

My wife, you said, shall walk this earth
    Queen of all women passing fair ;
Tall shall she be, with red-gold hair—
Such hair as once in Venice shone
On " dear dead " brows—and men shall own
Her mind than all her charms more worth ;
She shall wear lightly classic lore ;
She shall be poet, orator,
Painter, musician, all in one.


Your wife nor beauty boasts, nor grace,
Nor genius men should bow before,
Love's lamp alone illumes her face,
Kindness her voice its tones hath lent ;
What though her hair be flecked with grey,
Her eyes by sorrow clouded o'er,
Her head a little downward bent—
Poor head that wears no leaf of bay !—
You seem to love her more and more.

# THE SEASONS

Woods for the Spring! the stirring, **wakening**
  woods,
**Full of** dim glades that daily duskier grow,
**And arched recesses** where the blackbird builds,
**And** chants, full-voiced, his oft repeated stave.
O, for the cool fresh woods in early Spring!

Gardens for Summer! homely village plots,
Where roses clasp the long-arm'd apple-trees,
And columbines join hands with mint and **rue,**
While bees grow clamorous over beds of thyme,
And June is hastening to the longest day.

For Autumn, moorland, sun-warmed, wind-caressed;
Scant change from summer glory do **we know**
**On** the wide moor.  In the clear Autumn **air**
The lark resumes his interrupted song,
**And on the** distant hills the heather burns.

And what for winter ?   Why, the lone sea shore ;
The sandy waste puts forth nor bud nor leaf
For frost to smite.   No promise unfulfilled
Vexes us here ; the sea suffices us,
The patient, wise, companionable sea.

## IN THE CHURCHYARD.

B<sup>Y</sup> her grave to be, near the cypress tall,
    That, sentinel-like, keeps guard on the place,
She sat; then she rose from the low stone wall—
    The joy of living alight in her face—
And danced on the turf in her childish glee,
With never a thought of what should be.


Of what should be but a few years thence ;
    For the child so loved of us, Death loved too;
He stole from his shades, and her soul bore hence,
    Heavenward, we know, for our faith is true.
We laid her to rest by the cypress tree,
With many a thought of what should be.

Of what should be when this life were done,
     And the next one reached, we fitfully talked,
As back from her grave to our cold hearthstone,
     And desolate home, we, faltering, walked.
Thus talk we no longer ; yet dreams are free ;
We dream of what was, and no more may be.

# A SEALED LETTER.

You see this writing next my heart? Come nearer!
    *My* hand—why not? This is the sole **love-letter**
I ever penned.   'Twas sent to one far dearer
    **Than** stammering lips could tell.   I loved her
        better—
Such depth of feeling diffidence may cover—
Than many **a** bolder lover.


There came no answer to my passionate pleading :
    Death called my lady ere the **seal was broken ;**
Yet, for an hour—a lifetime by love's reading—
    She clasped this record dumb of vows unspoken.
**One took** it from her when he knew her sleeping
**And** gave it to my keeping.

O, heart of mine made pure by touch of paper
   *Her* heart has touched—nay, have her lips not
      kissed it ?—
Keep faithful guard, and when my life's dull taper
   Fails, if some curious hand approach, resist it !
Let her reclaim her own when we meet yonder ;
Will she be glad, I wonder ?

## TO ONE IN ITALY.

FROM lands beyond the sea,
    You ask a song of me,
Here in a cold grey clime where loves of youth
Seem half-forgotten ; where, in very truth,
My lute is well-nigh silenced ; where, at last,
My heart may grow as silent as my lute.
But if your touch—your warm and glowing finger,
Swept o'er its strings, erewhile so cold and mute,
You still might find some sad, sweet music linger
    In the poor chords and few,
    That you, and only you,
Have power to charm forth from the dying past.

## TO ONE IN ENGLAND.

Come hither, friend, from yonder wintry land;
    Come, walk with me beneath mine olive trees.
All Nature waits; the very roses store
Away their fullest tints your eye to please:
The sunlight, striking on the grey stone wall,
Desires your shadow; tender leaflets fall,
To hide the bareness of the marble floor
Your foot should press.　O Friend! for evermore
Must I and Nature wait you hand in hand?

# FLOWER OF LOVE.

*The heart is a garden, warmed by Hope, wherein grow the beauteous flowers of love, the like of which eye hath never seen.*

THE heart is a garden fair,
    And Hope is its sun ;
Flowers grow in it, many and rare,
    Yet prize we but one.


Whose bud like a sea-shell is fair,
    Its bloom like a flame ;
Its spices rise sweet in the air,
    And Love is its name.


There falls on our garden fair
    A frost—or a blight ;
Such weight can a frail flower bear ?
    Love dies in a night.

## MORIBUNDA.

*They know who work, not they who play, if rest is
sweet.*

FAREWELL to hope of Spring, of summer bloom ;
　　Farewell to love, the love of days long dead ;
I would not, if I could, lost joys resume ;
　　Too late for love, she said.


Farewell to sounds of earth, or harsh or sweet,
　　Voices that echo in an aching head :
Speed on, ye hours ! pass, pass with swifter feet !
　　Leave me to rest, she said.


Rest from the worldly ways *my* feet have trod,
　　A work-day world whence all delight hath fled ;
Poor pilgrim on life's weary, toilsome road,
　　The shrine is near ! she said.

Rest? should the soul in me soar swift away
   To sunshine, soul so long to darkness wed,
Rest will it be but to behold that ray,
   Day's very spring, she said.

## TO CRYSTAL.

HE that has made you his wife,
　　He that has given you his life,
Cold to the touch of your hand,
Passes to shadow-land.


Love you he did, faults and all ;
Now with his face to the wall,
Calm in a new, strange wise,
Deaf to your frenzy, he lies.


He, whose fresh fountains outburst
Ere you could utter " I thirst ; "
One little droop of your mouth
Once would have told him your drouth.

What ! you loved, too, do you say ?
Yours was a fire of one ray ;
Less than a ray, a mere spark
Struck from a flint in the dark.


Love is a tree that demands
Culture and warmth at our hands ;
You who put ice to its root,
Look not thereafter for fruit !

# GRIEF'S PHILOSOPHY.

"THE child is ill." She turned and stayed her hand
    Nor quite arranged the rose-wreath that she
      wore
  Set in her curls. Her small foot beat the floor ;
In thought she heard the music of the band
That summoned her to reign in fairyland :
    "O for one dance," she cried, "one wild waltz
      more ! "


"The child sleeps well." And, as she spoke she
    dreamed
  Of sorrows that had marred her life before
  She wedded wealth ; then, new things pondered
    o'er
She had but now begun to live, it seemed.
Swift from the glass again her bright eyes gleamed ;
    "One triumph more," she cried, "one triumph
      more!"

" The child is dead."   Harsh sound the brief words
    bore,
  As her returning foot the threshold pressed.
  Her frozen lips scarce moved—"At rest ! at rest!"
She climbed the stair, she pushed the chamber door,
She laid her rose-wreath on the baby's breast ;
   " One sorrow more," she moaned, " one sorrow
    more ! "

# MOIRA.

O FATE, whose finger spun the dull brown thread
    That, woven, makes the vesture of my life,
Bethink thee ! did no strand of rosy-red,
    No hint of Tyre, with sunset flushes rife,


No golden threadlet plead to be entwined
    Amongst the brown ?　What subtle harmonies
Of gold and colour might, therein enshrined
    Have leapt to light.　But thou saw'st otherwise.


And I must wear, with what poor grace I may,
    This sober garb amid the motley crowd
Who frolic merrily along Time's way,
    Until I fold it round me for a shroud.

# LILY.

### *Born December 31st.*

THE year is dying slowly. Faint and chilly,
    His last star burns. A group of maidens stand
Beside the city gates, with garlands fair,
To crown the blithe newcomer, who, with hair
**Flying, and** hurrying foot, will straight demand
Entrance of him who guards the iron-bound door.
"What! shall the dying year go forth unblest
"By bud or bloom, amid such bounteous store?
"Yield him one blossom ere he sink to rest!
"Behold! this fair, sweet thing men **call a lily,**
"I keep for him!" Thus spake the janitor.

## AMARANTH.

SHE cannot die ; her presence fills our home :
    Others can pass forgotten, but she had
A hundred points to hold the memory by,
Like rose-leaves snatched from summer to make glad
The senses in the wintry days to come,
When sunlight fades, and hearts grow chill and sad,
And thro' the ruined garden west winds sigh.

## "BEYOND THESE VOICES."

Few understood him ; many loved him well ;
    Courteous, clear-headed, no mean orator ;
    One, above all, well versed in Nature's lore,
Her power was on him, and beneath her spell


Wonders he saw.  In a dark world the East
    Guarded for him one little rift of gold ;
    The sternest rocky hill for him unrolled
A softening veil of purple amethyst.


For him the wind-tormented, wintry trees
    Glowed with a recollection of dead Junes,
    Birds in mid-autumn sang their nesting tunes,
Bare hedgerows flamed with flowers his eye to please.

And can such joys, like dreams that die with night,
    Be as they had not been ?　In that new sphere
    Wherein he moves, is earth no longer dear ?
Shall Nature minister to his delight


No more ?　And we ourselves, our hopes, our fears ?
    Surely he knows our projects of each day,
    Our suns that rise in gold and set in grey ;
Our mirth must move his mirth, our tears, his tears ?


We know not, nay, nor shall know, maybe not
    Until we too touch land, gain that vast shore
    Whose bounds Time's foot were powerless to
      explore.
As we pause, dazzled, new to that bright spot,


Suppose this man, with eyes like dawning day
    And face remoulded to its early prime,
    Full of great, sad, regretful thoughts sublime,
Should step forth, smiling in the old wise way,

Lay in our own his indolent, kind hand—
    Such warmth of welcome in his kindling eye
    That " Farewell goes out sighing," fain to die—
And bid us in : then, shall we understand ?

# A WHITE VIOLET.

BORN out of season; not when light winds play
With budding boughs, but when strong eddies
shake
The last leaves down.   November is as May
To us, for her dear sake.


Died in full summer, when white lilies tall
And clove carnations bloom; our senses ache
Remembering these.   Heavy thy footsteps fall,
July! for her dear sake.


Hers was a flower-like life, so brief, so dear!
Must earth's best flowers the briefest sojourn make?
Yea, but heav'n's blossoms flourish all the year;
Look up! for her dear sake:

Then, for your eyes and ears, a fuller note
  In all created nature shall awake ;
Song-birds shall warble forth from deeper throat,
  Joyful, for her dear sake.


Roses, long laid in ashes, shall revive,
  Violets their ancient sweetness shall retake ;
All things that be, in richer splendour live,
  Richer, for her dear sake.


And, each with other, you and yours shall vie
  In acts of love to those whose sad days break
In rayless gloom : so, joy shall underlie
  Your tears, for her dear sake.

# IN A LIGHTHOUSE.

WHAT! you would see the lighthouse, Sir?
    Forgive me if I am but slow
To hear; there's always such a stir
    At sea.   Besides, I'm old, you know.


Alone, Sir? Yes, save for a lad—
    They sent me one to share my watch
When....let that pass—a many I've had,
    Of youths, since then.   Aye, raise the latch,


And we'll go up.   My thoughts had flown,
    As you stood calling there below,
To one clear voice, that to my own
    Made joyous answer long ago.

Thanks ; when I sit my limbs are eased ;
  Such stairs ! Here's the machinery—
(Tell you my story ?  But too pleased)—
  By which the light is flashed to sea.


" A peaceful land ! "  On that my thought
  Was dwelling when I heard you speak ;
Three little words ; they're all I brought
  From church ashore on Sunday week.


" A peaceful land ! "  the parson said ;
  Not often do I go ashore ;
Idly I'd wandered, church-ward led
  By thoughts of one who nigh the door


Lies buried ; she I loved and lost
  Years since, my wife, a tender thing ;
We married when I gained this post,
  She left me ere the second spring.

Nature had nursed her; she had moved
   In country air since she was born;
All sounds and sights of earth she loved;
   Birds' songs, green hedgerows, waving corn.


I, selfish fool! God help me! I
   Who loved her, tore my meadowsweet
From her fair field to droop and die;
   No kind earth here to woo her feet.


Yet think what 'twas to have her! how
   Things that she breathed on took new grace;
She and her pot-flowers, all ablow,
   Made quite a glory in the place.


At first she, like her flowers, increased
   In beauty; brightly gleamed her eye.
" I'm seasoned well," she'd say in jest;
   " Not salter was Lot's wife than I ! "

Alas! they dwindled, she and they,
  "A little earth!" their silent plea;
They thirsted in the salt, salt spray,
  They shuddered at the creeping sea.


I lured her in my fishing-boat
  To sail, some twice or thrice, no more;
But all the hours we spent afloat,
  She kept her face fast set to shore.


She loved not sport—I mind me well—
  Shrank at the barking dog-fish din;
Screamed when, as bait for mackerel,
  I sliced their kindred's rainbow skin.


And many a time, on stormy nights,
  Her tender heart with fear was stirred,
As, following where I watched the lights,
  The clash of wind and wave she heard,

And caught her breath and, sighing, went
   Back to her room where no light was ;
She could not look while gulls, storm-spent,
   Beat themselves blind against the glass.


She faded, young.  I bowed my head,
   Crying, thro' tears, " God's ways are best !
Better by far my dove were dead,
   Than pining in this sea-bird's nest."


I hung above her, tried to catch
   One word for me.  No use !  She cried
For lilies from some shady patch
   Near the old home, fell back, and died.


Oh !  " Land at last ! "  The salt sea-mist
   Gathers no more before her eyes ;
She plucks Heav'n's lilies if she list,
   And roams at will thro' Paradise.

There, "no more sea ;" For barren, lean
　Unstable furrows ridged with foam,
Green meadows ; streams that wind between ;
　(A brook ran past her childhood's home).


So, when I heard "a peaceful *land*,"
　I pictured one by Jordan's banks.
She will be there, you understand—
　What ! going, Sir ? Good day ! and thanks.

## ARRÊTS D'AMOUR.

THREE sat apart in a wide window-seat
   O'erlooking Thames; three girls, Pearl, Star,
      and Dove;
The first was speaking. "Yes; extremes do meet
  Oft-times. The great brown hand of my tall love
Could toss me like a feather. O, tis sweet


" To know him bondslave to one small pale girl;
   To feel how potent are my charms on him;
They keep him constant. O'er this tendrilled curl,
   A shower would make short work of, what a hymn
Of praise he sings. Only to whisper "Pearl!"
   Or touch my hand, his honest eyes grow dim."

"Too constant is inconstant!" flashed out Star;
  "He loves one day your hair, the next your hand,
A third your figure; then your soft eyes are
  Sweeter than all.  If love I understand
Love for love's sake alone were better far.


"O'er vaunted constancy, I woo not thee!
  Between four eyes full many a witching look
May pass—but not the same two pairs for me:
  The *tête-à-tête* domestic who could brook?
Not I, forsooth!  Pearl could, perhaps, though she
  Might grow a **trifle weary if** the book


"Of life lay ever open at one page:
  Dove, now, wise child, loves calm; (if wisdom were
      were
But catching, or grew on us like old age,
  How wise *I* might be yet).  Come, Dove, declare
The thoughts that lurk behind that forehead sage!"

"Love—love I know not, lover having none,"
  Said Dove, "love language to my lips is thus
Strange; but if loved, wedded for love alone,
  I should be faithful found, I think.  To us
Women it seems so easy to enthrone


"One as our king.  I'd bow to mine, nor kick
  Against his mandates.  Poor, I'd work for him;
Amuse him when in health; nurse him when sick,
  Not shrinking from grief's cup though filled to brim;
Not flinching though God's hand to "dead" changed
            "quick."


"Depressing strain!  Tinkle of physic phial!"
  Laughed Star in scorn, and smote one pretty palm
Against the other.  "Slowly, round Time's dial,
  The hands would travel to such music.  Calm?
Stagnation!  Such a life indeed were trial.

"Hail, Pleasure!  Thee I'll worship; so thou please
    My ears with mirth, my eyes with beauteous things—
Laughter for those, jewels and silks for these—
    So I, poor drone, may soar on painted wings
Far over this dull throng of working bees."


"O, Star!" cried Dove, "O, wandering, fitful fire!
    Leave not our chimney-corner to go burn
On alien hearths!  Better by far to tire
    Of lighting up our loving eyes than turn
To dust and ashes on some distant pyre."


"Brief home affections!"  Sadly now spoke Star.
    "Where are our true, true friends of yesterday?
Dead, changed to us, or journeying hence afar;
    Their ghosts alone come up the moonlit way
Themselves trod singing.  Poor, mute ghosts they
                are!
    Snapped lute-strings yield more melody than they."

Silence ensued ; a silence that the girls
   Seemed loth to break. Evening fell, still and fair;
A time for thought. The low, red sun smote Pearl's
   Gold head to flame, just tinted Dove's pale hair,
And shot bright arrows through Star's dusky curls.


Soon, five shrill whistles from the river greet
   Pearl's ear, who from the room moves swift away,
Her love with prompt obedience to meet;
   Dove steals apart to meditate and pray ;
Alone, Star sits in the wide window-seat,
   Face dropt in hands, till night falls cold and grey.

## RIDUNA LYS.*

BORN in the isle that gave her her quaint name,
   Fair, wise as fair, and with a heart at ease
Was she, until one dolorous day there came
   A ship that brought strange gods from overseas.
   Gods? nay, mere mortal men and women; these
She deemed gods, seeing nothing to proclaim
   That feet of clay lurked 'neath their draperies.
She watched them land with eyes and cheeks aflame.


She, so close cloistered in that sea-girt spot,
   Mistook for prayer their worldly litany;
Hung on their lips, the claims of home forgot;
   Forgot all else save the wild hope that she
   Might please the cold blue eyes of one, and he
A king of men; thanked Heav'n that no dark blot
   Defaced a page in all her ancestry;
Played folly's game, "he loves me; loves me not."

   * **Riduna**; the Roman name for the island of Alderney.

Her father owned a little boat, wherein
　　Her pastime oft had been to sail or row;
But now each day with pleasures would begin,
　　That ended not with day, but seemed to grow.
　　No need for "pastime" in her full life now:
To steal an hour from her new god were sin;
　　She merged her thoughts in his, nor cared to know
Aught, save the way his looks and words to win.


That was her dream, as sweet as it was brief;
　　Doubt stirred in her; then came awakening.
Dry-eyed she saw—her proud soul scorned relief
　　Of softening tears—that man whom she called king
　　With his gay crew, make for the ship, whose wing
Was spread for flight.　One in her ear said "Thief!
　　"Your love to steal, and then aside to fling."
But deaf she was and mute with sullen grief.


She could not rest.　Down from the quay she flew,
　　Loosed boat—that ship to reach her only aim—

And gained the shadow that its tall side threw.
From overhead a voice—a woman's—came :
"Poor Ariadne of the savage name !
"Who'll dry the tears she weeps 'for one untrue' ? "
A man's voice answered with no note of shame,
"Some island Bacchus may; *I* follow *you*."


Homewards ! she lands :  Yon rock hides caves that she
Of old had shunned for fear.  Without demur
She enters one, lies down and smiles to see
The tide creep up.  Entranced, she cannot stir,
Though the small, stealthy shore-crabs climb on her,
In doubt what this strange, passive thing may be.
At last, one wave breaks on the rock's sharp spur,
And all her hair floats on the rising sea.

# THE POET TO A LADY

WHO HAD WISHED TO SEE HIM.

*Clément Marot.*

SHE, from reading of my lays,
    Loved me; then would see my face;
Saw me; liked me none the less,
For grizzling beard and swarthiness.
Ah! sweet spirit, high-born maid,
True the judgment you displayed;
Grown already grey, this shell
You behold—it is not I,
'Tis the jail wherein I dwell.
When my written words you read,
Reason guiding your bright eye,
Then you see myself indeed.

# MADONNA.

*Francesco Morone.*

A CHILD'S curved lip; a woman's thoughtful eyes;
    An oval face with look half proud, half-sweet;
A face as pure as some sheathed lily-bud
That, softly swaying to Sicilian airs,
Waits to blow wide—a snow-white, perfect flower,
Fit for the fingers of Persephone.

# MY HOUSEHOLD GODDESS.

### *A Burne-Jones Damsel.*

SILENCE she keeps.  Not even at Love's command
    Speaks she, but yields the mute applause of eyes
  To my outspoken fancies, wild or wise :
Nor music makes she, though her slender hand


Holds the tuned viol.  Grave, serene and fair
  She, all unstirred by vain imaginings,
  Suspends the bow above the soundless strings
And waits my pleasure on the " Golden Stair."

# LOVE AND DEATH.

### *G. F. Watts, R.A.*

THINK'ST thou, fond Love, to tear the awful pall
   From Death's dread face, his vanquisher to prove,
    Or pity in that icy breast to move?
White Death no pity knows for great or small.
What guard'st thou in thy citadel, that tall
   Thorn-studded briars defend?  Some wounded
       dove,
   Prey of thy pliant bow, whom thou, O Love!
Nursest to life with food ambrosial?


Vain conflict! vain endeavour!  Know that Death
   Holds thy pleach'd barriers but as blades of grass:
    Soon he will close with thee, yea, breast to breast,
And when—thine eyes o'erclouded, faint thy breath—
   Thou fall'st, 'mid rending garlands he shall pass
    Over thy prostrate body to thy nest.

## THE PEACEMAKER.

*Marcus Stone, R.A.*

Kiss and be friends!  Do love-bonds bring such
    woe
That you two souls should break them thus, and go
  (One with averted eyes as if, maybe
  Fearful the other's anxious looks to see)
By parted ways, with footsteps sad and slow?


In this sharp hour life's furnace is aglow;
Say, shall it shrivel you to dust, or show
   Your hearts pure gold?  The last?  Then, speedily
     Kiss and be friends!

Come, frown not ; copy Nature's smiles !   You owe
Her thanks to-day for tones and tints that grow
  Hourly more joyous ;  hues of flower and tree ;
  White lambs that leap upon an emerald lea ;
Would you supply the note of gloom ?   Ah ! no ;
        Kiss and be friends !

# A HAND AT WHIST.

"A HAND at whist! You'll be so kind?"
    My hostess murmurs from behind;
I take my seat with rueful face.
Right, left, two players fill the space;
Ladies, but somewhat tough of rind.


Angels and ministers of grace!
A goddess claims the vacant place:
    Takes—to my own I am resigned—
        A hand at whist.


What had I lost had I declined
This game abhorrent to my mind?
    A ruffled mass of creamy lace,
    That, swept from a round wrist, displays,
White, plump, with each blue vein defined,
        A hand—at whist.

## SHOULD AMY WALTZ.

SHOULD Amy waltz, I'd straight begin
        To steal the ball-room precincts in :
    My dancing days are o'er, but lo !
    Such grace her airy movements show,
To lose the sight were surely sin.


With myriad charms my glance to win,
Up-curling lashes, saucy chin,
        Dark hair, and eyes that mock the sloe ;
                *Should* Amy waltz ?


Ah ! me, each rhythmic twirl and spin
Might bear a lesson writ therein.
        How old we poor outsiders grow ;
        *I* am past waltzing, well I know.
    No matter !   I'd not care a pin,
                Should *Amy* waltz.

# THIS BOOK OF MINE.

THIS book of mine, when curled perukes
 Were worn 'twas printed. Earls or dukes
 (Princes are bibliophiles to-day)
 Might buy this volume, who can say?
Now Fortune bids me sell my books.


Its tattered state the hope rebukes;
Once an *édition de luxe*,
 Now it is verging on decay,
    This book of mine.


How it recalls past summers! Brooks
Murmur, larks sing; loud caw the rooks;
 Pink petals fall; hands fair as they
 Drop them among these pages grey:
Let be! too like a friend it looks,
    This book of mine.

# I WAS A ROSEBUD IN JUNE.

*Appéna se può dir: " Questa fu rosa ? "*

I WAS a rosebud in June,
   Dewy, and fragrant and fair;
Now, my poor petals are strewn.

Thrushes were singing in tune,
   There, where I scented the air:
I was a rosebud in June.

Pluck'd, say a sun-round too soon,
   Ere my deep heart could lie bare:
Now, my poor petals are strewn.

How can I Fate importune?
　Where is my loveliness? where?
I was a rosebud in June.


No man could count me a boon
　Fit to bestow on his fair,
Now my poor petals are strewn.


Dead, ere morn melts into noon!
　What is there left?　To declare,
She was a rosebud in June;
Now, her poor petals are strewn.

# THIS DAY.

*Pensa che questo dì mai non raggiorna.*

THINK! on this rapturous day, clear after rain,
  When bees hum loud and roses open wide
And birds chant anthems, have we glorified
The day by one small act, or striven to gain
Ease for ourselves?   Wept we at one friend's pain?
  Balm to one sufferer's wounds have we applied,
  Or like the Levite coldly turned aside?
"Think, that this day will never dawn again!"


Think this; not sadly—sadness chains the free;
  Among the tombs to linger is not meet—
    But onward press where good men walked before,
Till on the shores of some far Galilee
  We sit, content, at our great Master's feet,
    Watching the dawn that darkens nevermore.

# PASTOR BONUS.

M<small>Y</small> sheep I know and love ; no lambs too young
    For me to care for; guide their stumbling feet;
  Teach them to crop the tender herbage sweet;
Carry them, when they fall rough briars among.
Did I not leave for these the heavenly throng,
    The glories of the jewel-paven street ;
  Change angels' music for their plaintive bleat,
Singing, myself, on earth, a shepherd's song ?


My sheep I love.  But am I loved of mine ?
    Mayhap their lines in pleasant places fall;
      They need me not.  Let be! A time may come,
Some night so dark not ev'n the pale stars shine,
    They wander, lost.  Alone, I hear their call :
      Then do I haste to lead my strayed flock home.

# THE SOUL'S TEMPLE.

*I will search Jerusalem with candles.*

CLEANSE thou the temple of thy soul! Fling wide
　　Doors, windows. Sweep the walls. Let sun-
　　beams play
　Where hang the fungus growths of many a day;
Scan each small nook where noxious things may
　　　hide;
The slippery snake, Deceit, the blind worm, Pride,
　The spider, Avarice, make thou haste to slay;
　Brush cobwebs with relentless hand away;
Let no dark spot remain unpurified!


Swept? Garnished? It is well; now take good
　　heed,
　Thy house made fit to bear God's searching light,

What souls thou sufferest pass the threshold o'er.
Spurn the seven wicked spirits.   Yea, indeed,
  Smite if they enter.   Watch: on some blest night,
  Angels may steal in through the open door.

# EARTH-NOTES.

Dɪᴅ we believe that thoughts of us still move
　　Those loved ones who have joined the heavenly
　choir—
　That noble deeds of ours (how rare!) inspire
To fuller harmony their notes of love:
That faults of ours (how frequent!) can, inwove
　　Into that music, snap the harpist's wire,
　　Untune the white-robed player's golden lyre—
Such discord-makers we were loth to prove.


Ah! could a victory o'er ourselves be won!
Yet not alone such warfare dare we try:
　Tuning our voices till they reach His throne
Who valiant is, yet tender—Lord! we cry,
　Stand on our side! So shall we, bolder grown,
Fight sin, as Christian fought Apollyon.

# THE DREGS OF THE CUP.

WHAT do we give to God ?   Our best or worst ?
   Our gold—the gold of social state, the price
  Of pleasure ? or, sweet gift of sacrifice,
Our frankincense ?  (Whoso shall quench the thirst
Of one in need, tho' last, shall e'en be first.)
   Our myrrh ?   Or keep we back the gold and spice
   For our rich burial, when Death's hand of ice
Grips us, wide scattering all our wealth accursed ?


O, patient God ! when we, at last, with tears,
   Shall seek thee, slow awakening out of sleep ;
     Stunned with a fall from our once lofty place,
With eyes of seeing tired, of hearing, ears ;
   Scarce strong enough to lift loth limbs to creep
     Close to Thy feet—avert not Thou Thy face !

www.ingramcontent.com/pod-product-compliance
Lightning Source LLC
Chambersburg PA
CBHW020047030726
47499CB00007B/2626